ROYAL TROUBLE
the SINISTER REGENT

HOPE ERICA SCHULTZ
Illustrated by Jeff Crosby

CBAY Books
Dallas, Texas

The Sinister Regent (Royal Trouble #1)

Text Copyright © 2018 by Hope Erica Schultz
Illustrations by Jeff Crosby.

For more information, write:
CBAY Books
PO Box 670296
Dallas, TX 75367

Children's Brains are Yummy Books
Dallas, Texas
www.cbaybooks.blog

Paperback ISBN: 978-1-944821-32-6
ebook ISBN: 978-1-944821-33-3
Kindle ISBN: 978-1-944821-34-0
PDF ISBN: 978-1-944821-35-7

For CPSIA information, please see:
cbaybooks.blog/cpsia-information/

Printed in the United States of America.

For Joy, who waited not-so-patiently for the story to be complete.

Jes bounced on her sister's bed, just missing the pile of dresses Alex was packing. She frowned, kicking her worn boots against the sideboard. "I wish I was going, too."

Alex snorted. "No, you don't. It will be dressing up every day and boring dinner parties and getting introduced to boys who either can't dance or have nothing interesting to say."

Jes shrugged, running her hand over a blue silk dress. "I like dresses. They're not as good to run and climb in as normal clothing, but they're fun sometimes."

"You couldn't wear your boots under these."

Jes shuddered and let go of the dress. "But why

do *you* have to go?"

Their mother poked her head in from the hallway. "Because she's sixteen and old enough to get introduced into Society. She needs to see if she enjoys this kind of life before she rejects it. She can't refuse her birthright until she's eighteen, so she has two years to decide if she'll stay a princess, and be heir to East Waveborn, or choose to be a commoner instead."

Queen Eris of East Waveborn was shorter than Alex, but with the same auburn hair and green eyes as both her daughters. Jes stood up as tall as she could, but her mother was still just a little taller.

"I'd rather be a commoner. I think this royalty business is a royal pain," Jes grumbled. "I have to stay, but I'm not in charge of anything. And it's school break, so I won't even have my friends around!"

The queen smiled. "You'll have that adviser from Alsandia to stay with you. Technically, I suppose she'll be your regent if anything comes up, but I'll bet that Gregor sent someone nice. It makes sense that he wants someone experienced to help you."

Gregor was King Gregor of Alsandia, a college friend of their parents and the reason Jes was stuck being a Princess. It had been his bright idea to make the islands into tiny kingdoms and give this one to her parents. *He'd better have sent someone nice.*

"And that reminds me," Queen Eris said. "You need to get in your reading while we're gone. History and science. I ordered some new books."

Jes took the books from her mother's hands and looked them over dubiously. "But it's *vacation.*"

Her mother snorted. "You haven't been reading much of anything except fiction lately. You need a grounding in reality."

Jes thumbed through the top book, *A Brief History of the Known World.* "Hey, there's a section about the islands! 'And then Crown Prince Gregor did summon from across the Kingdoms heroes to combat the strange evil lurking in the Western Sea. Mighty warriors and warlocks, sorceresses and scholars, all came to face the dreaded foe.'"

Queen Eris snatched the book away from her. "So much for reality."

Alex hid her face, but she couldn't stop her laughter. "Warlocks, Mom!"

Their mother glowered a moment and then sighed.

"It wasn't like that at all. We were just friends of Gregor's from college. People mistook Melia for a sorceress because they didn't understand science. The closest thing we had to a warrior was your Uncle Phineas, and he usually just talks people into doing what he wants. We were … just looking into things for Gregor when we ran into the pirates. And then we ended up raising the islands back up out of the ocean, and Gregor appointed each of us the rulers of one of them to keep the big countries from fighting over who owned them."

She pushed the hair back from Jes's eyes and smiled. "You and your sister both know that ruling here just means that all the people who choose to live here now are our responsibility. It's our job to make sure that they are safe and that they have at least a chance to be happy."

"And that's why I have to go," Alex said to Jes. "I don't know if I want to be a ruler here after Mom and Dad step down. It's still my job to know what I'll be getting into if I do decide to rule. Do you understand?"

Jes kicked the floor, looking down. "I'm not a baby, you know. I'm nine."

"Well, you'll have *Everyday Alchemy* and *A Beginner's Guide to Steam* to keep you busy while we're gone," Mom told her. "At least science can be counted on not to embellish things."

Jes grimaced. "Wonderful."

"Cheer up, Bean Sprout. We'll be back before you know it." Alex held out her hand, revealing two gold earrings. "I'll let you play with my earrings while I'm gone. I'll even hide the right one for you before I leave."

Mother looked like she couldn't decide whether to object or laugh, and Jes slipped on the left earring quickly. A birthday present from Queen Melia and her son Donal, the right picked up sound and transmitted it to the left. Technically, it was a tool for spying. Alex liked to use them for hide and seek.

"Go see if Mrs. Clemens needs help with lunch," Alex advised. "I'll hide the other one while you're there."

Jes opened her mouth to argue—her family would be leaving after lunch, for five whole days!—then closed it again at a look from her mother. "See you at lunch," she said instead and let herself out of the door. She dropped the books off in her own room, then headed for the main stairs.

The stone castle had been underwater for centuries, the rock smoothed and oddly pitted, and none of the rugs and wall hangings could hide how old the place really was. It was also huge—thirty-seven bedrooms for a family of four.

Mom and Dad had filled it up some by using many of the rooms for the island's school—which meant Jes had no excuse to ever be late for class. They had a housekeeper, Mrs. Clemens, and six maids, three groundskeepers, and a pair of footmen, but there were still rooms that stayed empty most of the time.

The main staircase from the third floor to the first (you had to take other stairs to get to the second floor) was made of bone-white marble. The banister was new, polished wood and gilt, and Jes used to love to slide down it. She had given it up, mostly, now that she was getting older. She tramped down the stairs instead.

The kitchens were in the far back of the first floor. Mrs. Clemens was chef as well as housekeeper. Sometimes, she was also hair untangler, clothes patcher, and secret keeper.

Right now, she was taking bread out of the enormous brick oven. She paused, pushing a strand of graying hair back from her round face, and smiled.

"What trouble are you up to now, Princess?"

It was much more a nickname than a title, and Jes smiled as she pulled a wooden stool up to the gray stone counter. "Not much. I just wish that they didn't have to go."

Mrs. Clemens nodded. "It's hard to be left. Sometimes, though, it's just as hard to be the one to go. Your father hates these trips; your mother would enjoy them if she didn't have to watch every blessed word she said, and your sister has got to be nervous. She's been swimming in the shallows, and now she's being tossed out into deep water."

It was strange, thinking about it from other people's point of view. Jes frowned, considering. She'd been born on East Waveborn and had visited the other islands, but never the mainland. What was the mainland like?

"How did you come here, Mrs. Clemens?" she asked suddenly.

Mrs. Clemens laughed. "Me? I was a pirate, lass,

about the age your mother is now. It was hard work, but it paid. I was navigator under Dark Mathis when he went up against your parents and the others and lost. Most places, they just killed pirates on sight, but that group didn't believe in killing, no matter what stories you hear. If there was violence and treachery, it was on our side. Dark Mathis they dealt with somehow—I never asked—but the rest of us? We got a choice of a share of the money onboard that ship or a few acres of land here. I don't like farming, so I took the money and then asked your mother for a job."

Jes stared openmouthed until Mrs. Clemens handed her a slice of apple. She took a bite then looked up again. "Did you fight and everything?"

"With pistols, cutlasses, cannons, and most importantly, with my head. So yes, 'and everything.'"

Jes finished her apple and shook her head. "Then why be a housekeeper? You could still be off having adventures!"

Mrs. Clemens laughed softly and turned back to the stove. She stirred a pot of stew and looked back over her shoulder. "Sometimes, smaller adventures are more fun. I wrestle with numbers for your parents, conquer recipes, subdue whole classes with a look and a wooden spoon. Even better, I go to bed warm and safe—and wake up the same way." She pulled down a serving board and began cutting the fresh bread. "It's hard to believe at your age, but the best part of an adventure is getting home afterwards."

Jes tried not to complain at lunch. Her father, King Willem, had a tight look around his blue eyes, like he was facing something he'd rather avoid. "Airship, hmm?" he asked.

"Apparently, Gregor's sending the regent here in one, so it just makes sense that we take it back," Mom answered, patting their father's hand.

"I can't wait to fly on an airship!" Alex crowed, then winced. Jes suspected that Mom had kicked her under the table.

"I'm sure I'll get to ride in one eventually," Jes said, shrugging. "I hope you have a good time."

Mom's smile made her feel happy about the almost lie.

Alex chatted a little about things she hoped to see—a wax museum and the indoor water garden of

Darrius Hall and an entire street that sold nothing but shoes. Jes, who had been interested in the wax museum and water garden, shuddered at the idea of shopping.

There was a distant clap from the front door knocker as the table was being cleared. Dad jumped a little, and his guarded look came back, but Mom smiled.

"The airship must be here. Why don't we go see?"

They were in the breakfast room, where they always ate as a family. The oaken table and chairs would have held triple their number, but it was still tiny compared to the actual dining room. That room held the entire school for lunch, with room left over.

Alex touched her earlobe meaningfully. Jes brightened, remembering, and pushed gently on her single earring, turning it on.

Her family's feet clattered on the stone floors of the corridor, while Jes's boots made barely any sound. She thought of five days squished into sharp, noisy shoes. *Maybe staying behind isn't such a bad thing.*

Three people waited beside a very uncomfortable

looking footman. A pleasant, dark-skinned man in uniform was obviously the airship captain. Beside him stood a tall, imposing woman with black hair and sharp features. At the end was a little mouse of a man with graying hair and a nervous tic in his left cheek.

The woman swept into a low curtsy. "Your Majesties. I am Lady Umber, here to keep your younger child company while you are gone." She rose and looked them over, one eyebrow raised, then frowned. "I was told that you had two daughters?"

Jes felt herself flush. Alex opened her mouth, and Mother took a step forward, making a motion like a sword cut with her hand. "Indeed, we do. Our younger daughter, Princess Jesireen of East Waveborn, will, we are sure, be interested in your counsel."

I will never like her. I am never going to the mainland if they act like that, and I wish Mother would cut her head off. Jes didn't allow herself to look down at the tunic, hose, and boots that had made this stranger doubt her gender. She pretended that she was Mother and looked Lady Umber in the eye, nodding without smiling. "Welcome to East

11

Waveborn, Lady Umber. And your companion?"

Lady Umber looked uncomfortable and waved a hand toward the mousy gentleman. "My secretary, Mr. Wilson."

"Mr. Wilson." Jes nodded again, still not smiling. Alex was giving her their secret victory sign, and Father looked both proud and perturbed.

"Thank you, Captain, for delivering Her Ladyship here," Mother said, rather less icily. "We'll be ready to leave in just a moment." She turned and held out her arms to Jes, who ignored Lady Umber and her secretary to hug her back, hard.

"Good girl," Mother whispered. "Rough start, but I think she knows who's in control."

Alex hugged her next, then Father, and then they were out the door. Jes took a deep breath and turned back to her unwelcome companions.

"You must be tired. Franz will show you up to your rooms. Would you prefer a tray there or to come down to supper?"

Poor Franz, the footman, who had never witnessed such formality in his years at the castle, hid his face behind his hand and cleared his throat.

"A tray would be best for tonight," Lady Umber

agreed. "I hope you will call on me with even the smallest concern."

Jes nodded. "I will certainly remember your presence," she said truthfully. "Until tomorrow, then."

She turned and went up the main staircase to her room, where she punched her pillows until she was calm. *If this is being royalty, I don't want it.*

She did not cry herself to sleep. Her eyes might have been bothered by allergies, and she might have nodded off for a nap for a moment, but she wouldn't let a disagreeable person drive her to tears. Still, she woke up when sound began coming through the earring.

"Is it taken care of?" Lady Umber demanded.

"Yes," Mr. Wilson replied. "The airship was shot down."

"Shot down? It was supposed to explode. People can survive a sea landing."

"No one will survive. They're twenty miles from the nearest land. The girl is the only heir now, and you're the regent."

A feminine snort. "She's not going to be as easy as we were told, but she's still a child. Besides, if this island is too much trouble, we can always sink it again as a warning to the other three."

Jes held her breath, wondering if she still napped after all. Surely, they didn't mean—her parents, dead? Alex? They were willing to sink her island?

She remembered Aunt Anya talking to her mother late one night. *A hostage is already dead. Nothing you do can make that worse. Maybe, just maybe, you can help.*

Mrs. Clemens's voice echoed in her head. *Remember, in any crisis, you can always think of one good thing to do. While you're doing it, you'll think of another.*

First, she could stop the island from sinking. Second, she could get herself away, so she couldn't be used against her people. She'd have to warn someone—Mrs. Clemens—about what was going on. And she'd have to get word to someone she could trust.

If Gregor sent her, who can I trust?

Spare clothes went into a pack, along with some tools. She snuck down the back staircases to the kitchen. Preparations were underway for dinner, but the room was briefly empty, so she snuck through to the larder. Bread, cheese, and dried fruit went into her pack, along with a flask of ginger water.

She whirled around at a slight sound and sighed in relief at the sight of Mrs. Clemens.

"Princess Jes, what are you up to?" Title, not nickname. Mrs. Clemens looked like she was withholding judgment but suspected shenanigans.

"I overheard Lady Umber talking," Jes confessed. "She arranged to have the airship shot down. My—" She broke off, blinked hard, then went on. "She's willing to sink the island. I need to stop her."

It sounded preposterous. Just for a second, Jes questioned again whether she'd dreamed it. Then Mrs. Clemens nodded slowly. "I worked too many years with blackguards not to suspect that there was something off about her. Who are you taking with you?"

"Nobody. I don't know who might be working with her. King Gregor sent her! Maybe he knows, maybe he doesn't, but I can't risk it." Jes pulled herself up as tall as she could. "This is my country now. I won't let anyone hurt it."

Mrs. Clemens sighed. "I'll cover for you for as long as I can—you were up early, they just missed you, I'll be sure to pass on a message when I see you. You ... you be safe, Jes. You'll be going below?"

Jes nodded. The tunnel system was damp, but it was her only chance to go unnoticed. It was also where she needed to go to keep her kingdom safe.

Donal's mother, Queen Melia, had explained it to her once. Some ancient people had once used volcanic vents to raise and lower the different islands for their own purposes. It was impossible to tell if they had been used as farmland before, but it had taken years of special crops to clear the salt so the land could be fertile. Even if every single person made it off safely—*impossible*—the kingdom's livelihood would be gone if their island was submerged.

Mrs. Clemens stood guard as Jes took a candle and slipped through the larder to the root cellar. A trapdoor there led her down into caverns that were natural rather than manmade. At the bottom of the stairs was an armful of torches wrapped in oilcloth to keep them dry. Jes lit a torch with the candle, then blew the candle out. Two more torches went into her pack, to light from the first.

The torch's light flickered eerily over water droplets on the stone walls, and she could hear her own breathing. Jes set her teeth, and stepped forward towards the darkness ahead. She stopped at a sound from the earring, but it was just footsteps going by the room. *Good to know it has that kind of a range.*

The tunnel sloped down for a while. Jes sang for a few minutes, until she realized that she'd never hear anyone else over it if they were following her. Her feet made almost no noise in their soft boots. She could hear water dripping, reminding her that she was below the ocean here. If the tunnels flooded, she would drown.

The smoke from the torch made her nose itch, and sometimes a piece of ash would land on her hand, leaving a tiny burn. Old, dead barnacles dotted the walls, reminders from the centuries when this place had been underwater. There was some silt on the tunnel floor, some dried algae, some bones of unlucky fish. She imagined swimming through the tunnels instead of walking. It would be dark. She added a glowing light in her hand, then imagined she was a mermaid to make it all easier.

"If there were really warlocks, they could just imagine things into being," she told the torch. The flames burned on, uninterested. "Of course, if Lady Umber was a warlock, we'd already have lost. The real way is probably better."

She stopped after about an hour to have a drink of the ginger water and a bite of the cheese. Her only measurement of the time was the torch, and it had burned about a third of the way down. She remembered that they were supposed to last three hours each, and she hoped the two more she'd taken would be enough.

The first torch was almost gone when Jes reached the little spit of land that powered the vents. Back when her parents and the others had come to fight the pirates, it had been the only part of the island network still above water. Dark Mathis had had his pirate base on the tiny island above, using the higher caverns to hide treasure and guns and supplies. He hadn't realized the true purpose of the caverns.

Jes lit a second torch from the first and set the last of the dying torch into a wall holder. She took a deep breath, then started up the long flight of stairs. She could tell when she got to the part that had never submerged. The walls were different, a lighter gray without the water's touch. The mechanism was off to one side, a collection of stone and strange metal that looked like decorations. No one before Melia had guessed that it was more than that. It was the most powerful machine in the world.

Whoever planned this knows about the controls, Jes realized. *Not just that there's a way to do it but details about how they work. Otherwise, how would they know that you can sink just one of the islands?*

The power it took to sink the islands took time to build, just as the power to raise them had. Uncle Phineas liked to talk about the blend of fast talk and action they had used to hold the pirates off while the vents filled to the point where Melia could open them. Chris's parents, King Darby and Queen Lily, had used everything from smoke bombs to channeled lightning as delaying tactics, and Father had done something with soap and sheepskins that nobody would tell her about. Now she was the one delaying.

Everyone knew how steam could be used to

move pistons, generating power to run things like trains. Miniaturized systems that could power things as small as her fist were much more complicated. This was wildly different—steam technology on such a huge level that whole islands could rise and fall. There was no man-made fire in the world vast enough for this. The islands used a volcano instead.

The temperatures that melted rock were so hot that humans would be vaporized, but the lava was far away under the ocean floor. The steam was contained in huge chambers there, and could be released to power the great machine in a matter of minutes when they were full. If the steam was let out, however, it would take a long time for it to build up again.

Step one. She opened the safety valve for the volcanic vents fully. Queen Melia said the only downside to leaving it open was that a fifth island was likely to form over the vent, off to the north west, after a few decades. Jes could live with that. Even if the vent was fully closed now, it would take about a day to get the power all the way back up.

Step two. Jes brought out her tools and started individually sabotaging the controls that would sink each of the islands. It could be fixed, but that also would take hours.

Step three. Jes closed her eyes and breathed for a minute, going over the idea in her mind. If someone came to this chamber, they could undo her work. Unless the chamber was underwater.

The previous level of sea water hadn't reached the chamber, but adjusting that was easy enough. More difficult was setting up the failsafe. Jes decided that the failsafe would be anyone entering this chamber at all. Coming through, from above or below, would cause the tunnels to flood; the spit of land would still exist, but the chamber and the caverns below would be full. Since they were all below sea level anyway, that took no power—just an opening of doors.

It wasn't as clean a plan as Father would have preferred—he preferred contingency plans to his contingency plans—but it would work.

Did you have a contingency plan to getting shot out of the sky? She hoped fervently that he had.

She headed back down the stairs to the tunnels, pausing at the bottom to think. Protecting the islands had been the first priority, but now she had to find help. She used the burned-out torch to sketch with soot on the stone floor. To the east was the mainland, and the Kingdom of Alsandia where her parents had grown up and King Gregor ruled now. There were other countries on the mainland, but too far away to be helpful. Next were the islands—her own, East Waveborn, was the closest to Alsandia, but still a long ride by ship or a few hours by airship. Her parents' friends and Mom's sister were the rulers of the other Waveborn islands.

Dad said that the younger Waveborn royal kids were a direct result of Alex being a cute toddler. Whatever the reason, all four of the ruling families had had a child in the same year, and they'd grown up like cousins. Amalia, who lived in North Waveborn with Aunt Anya and Uncle Phineas, was her cousin by blood, too. Chris lived with his parents, King Darby and Queen Lily, in South Waveborn. Donal lived with his mother, Queen Malia, in West Waveborn.

Any of them would, and could, help her. It was habit more than anything that made Jes turn north towards her cousin Amalia. Aunt Anya always listened, no matter how weird a story was, and

Uncle Phineas kept his sense of humor no matter how dreadful things were.

Jes settled her pack onto her shoulders and took the tunnel to the north.

Breaking into North Waveborn was much harder than leaving East Waveborn had been.

Her first clue that the way was booby-trapped was a slightly higher pile of silt on the floor in front of her. Jes tapped it carefully with one foot, then sprang back as an axe came out of the wall just in front of her. There was a smiley face painted on it.

That's a nice welcome. She moved around the axe carefully and studied the path in front of her with more respect. Her second torch was getting low, and she ought to be getting close, but if the torch went out …

Jes pulled the third torch from her pack and lit it from the second. With one in each hand, she could see more clearly. Hopefully, she wouldn't drop both of them.

There were no barnacles on the stone to her left. Jes scowled, looking at the wall. She had seen sections without barnacles during her journey, but on the tunnel wall to her right, they were clustered quite thickly. She looked carefully at the blank wall, inching forward.

She heard a tiny creaking sound, and then knife-sharp barnacles shot out of the right-hand wall toward her. She ducked instinctively, and a pit in front of her opened up. She crouched on the edge, rocking back and forth between the floor and whatever lay below her in the pit. The smaller torch dropped from her hand into the pit. Before the torch went out, the light showed sharpened sticks and another drawing of a grinning face at the bottom.

Jes pushed herself back from the brink and swore. She tried out every phrase she had heard, and by the time she ran out of curses—after "Son of a one-eyed newt!"—she felt a little better. *Amalia and I are going to have a talk about this.* It had to be Amalia, her cousin. Aunt Anya and Uncle Phineas wouldn't have added insult to the injury of the traps.

There were a few more traps on the way. A couple of darts impaled her torch, and during the upslope, she avoided an oil patch designed to drop her on fist-sized jacks with sharpened ends. By the time she got within sight of the stairway out of the tunnels, she had been through her list of curses twice.

She sidestepped a net trap, ducked beneath a falling sword with a banner proclaiming OUCH!, and regarded the stairs up with suspicion. They were stone, so unlikely to give way beneath her. The walls could have been modified, however, and she poked carefully with a stick she'd taken from the pit trap.

She almost missed the motion sensors on the left, the response was so subtle. The third step triggered something she couldn't see, then the ninth step caused a sweeping metal rod to come out from the right.

"She has to be able to come down here," Jes muttered to herself. She waited for the trap to reset, then triggered first the ninth step then the third step. Nothing happened. She waited for the quick click that meant the trap had again reset, then hit the ninth step again. Still nothing.

"I can't believe she's patient enough for this."

Jes waited, triggered the ninth step, and walked up past the third to the sixth step and waited. After the click, she took a deep breath and walked up the rest of the stairs.

The trapdoor at the top had the same latch as her own, and she eased the door open a careful inch, listening. She could hear the clink and splash of dishes being washed. People were talking, too far away for her to make out any words. The scent of roasting chicken and baking bread made her stomach growl. She inched the trapdoor up just enough to scramble through. Her last torch was nearly dead; she blew it out and threw it back down.

She was in a storeroom that smelled strongly of vinegar. Jars of pickled vegetables filled the shelves, and the barrels were crusted with brine. Light came dimly from a high window and more brightly from the half-open door. Jes slipped behind a barrel and checked that the trapdoor was closed behind her.

Whom to trust? Was anyone here involved with the conspiracy? Jes chewed her lip and decided that even if no one else was involved, anyone who saw her could give her away. She had to find one of her family.

She'd been to North Waveborn before. She

closed her eyes briefly to picture the layout of the castle. From the sounds, she guessed the storeroom she was in was just off the kitchens. The main stairs were too visible, so Amalia preferred the servants' staircases. She'd shown them to Jes on the last visit.

Jes crept to the door. Footsteps were moving away, and she took a breath before scooting through. The nearly hidden stairs were on her right, and she scurried up them, grateful for the silence of her boots.

She paused in the shadows at the top of the stairway and held her breath. It was quiet except for the sound of her heart beating. She looked both ways, then sprinted down the hallway. She paused in Amalia's doorway and put her ear to the door. Nothing.

The door was unlocked, and she darted inside. Practice swords were scattered over a four-poster bed, with two more crossed on a white bureau. Blue curtains the same shade as the bed canopy went to the floor, and Jes darted behind one at a slight sound.

Someone stomped into the room, followed by the more sedate clatter of heeled shoes. Jes peeked out cautiously and saw Amalia scowling up at a taller figure.

"No, I don't intend to 'dress' for dinner, although you are welcome to do so. I'd just like a little quiet time, if you don't mind." There was the pause that usually meant that Amalia was going to lie. "I may have a headache coming on."

Amalia never had headaches, and she'd never submitted to quiet time even when she had a concussion. A feeling of dread settled over Jes.

"Then certainly you must rest, Your Highness," Lady Umber's voice answered, and Jes caught a glimpse of her before pulling back behind the curtain. *Do they have a second airship? How else could she get here so fast?*

The door closed, and Amalia knocked practice swords to the ground and landed on her bed, kicking her heels against the frame.

Jes tapped very quietly on the window behind her curtain, waited a moment, and then tapped again. She heard the bed creak, then the quieter sound of Amalia approaching. Amalia pushed aside the curtain, a practice sword in one hand.

"Oh!" Amalia tilted her head, looking her over.

"Jes, what are you doing here?"

Amalia was brown skinned and brown haired, like her father, and full of such life and energy that Jes often felt like a ghost next to her. "Shh! I need to talk to your parents. Something terrible is going on."

Amalia snorted. "Tell me about it. My parents got called to some important thing on the mainland, and King Gregor sent *that* woman to be my regent while they're gone. She's just awful!"

Jes nodded. "I know. Lady Umber showed up just after lunch. When did she get here?"

Amalia shook her head. "Mine is Lady Grey, and she's been here since mid-morning. This is the first I've gotten away from her all day."

Jes frowned. "But it's the same woman. Same face, same voice. Twins, maybe?" She shook her head. "Anyway, that's not the important part. I overheard mine talking with her secretary. They've shot down my family's airship, and she plans to rule as my regent. And she said if my island didn't cooperate, they'd just sink it."

Amalia stared at her a moment, then dropped the wooden practice sword and lifted a real sword from the wall. "Over my dead body." She leapt up to her bed and lifted the sword high so that it almost touched the blue canopy. "We'll fight them all!"

Jes sighed. "I don't think your parents would advise a frontal assault right now."

Amalia looked disappointed. She lowered the sword and hopped back down. "Espionage?" she asked hopefully.

"Remove potential hostages first," Jes said firmly. "That means us."

Amalia sighed. "Fine. Let me ring for a tray for supper and then ask not to be disturbed. Then we can head out. I'm bringing my sword, though."

"Of course."

Jes hid behind the curtain again while the tray was delivered. They shared the meal, which worked well since Jes wouldn't eat meat pie and Amalia didn't like chicken. Amalia packed up her essentials—two daggers, a flask of oil with a fire-starter, and double handfuls of marbles and smaller jacks—she called them caltrops—in their own bags. Jes got her to add a change of clothes, and they were off.

Amalia was prepared. A rope ladder was hidden behind her bed just in case she was ever locked in. They were discussing whether to use it or sneak down to the kitchens when Jes heard a sound through her earring. She held up one hand and concentrated, but she only heard a door open, a few steps, and then the door closing again.

"This thing is incredible," she murmured.

"What thing?" Amalia asked, examining the rope ladder for weaknesses.

"My—Alex's earring." She explained briefly. "I think we'll be less noticeable on the servants' stairs than trying to break back into the castle, don't you?"

Amalia tossed the ladder back behind her bed. "It should be late enough. I'll go first, since there's no trouble if I'm caught."

They reversed Jes's earlier trip with Amalia in the lead, but the kitchens were empty, the fires banked. The jars of pickles looked like they might contain scarier things in the near darkness, and Jes imagined disembodied heads floating, watching them. She changed the mental image to Lady Umber's severed head and immediately felt better.

Amalia led the way into the deeper darkness of the stairs and paused to light a torch once the trapdoor had closed behind them. "I wish I had time to set traps for anyone following us."

Jes grimaced as she stuck three more torches into her pack. "The traps you have are plenty."

Amalia shrugged. "Well, you got past them all. After all this is over, you'll have to show me where I went wrong."

Jes wasn't sure if Amalia had realized that there might not be an "after." She just nodded and let Amalia lead the way until they were clear of the traps.

It felt like she had been walking for days by the time they reached the turnoff for South Waveborn. Jes hadn't worn a watch, but it had to be getting on to midnight, and she'd left perhaps an hour after lunch. She felt herself starting to lag and was grateful for Amalia's energy.

"So, after we enlist Chris's parents, I say we mount a two-pronged attack through the tunnels to free both of our islands," Amalia proposed. "But do we kill them or arrest them so they can be executed formally?"

Jes was usually a lot less bloodthirsty than her cousin, but she paused to seriously consider the choice. The earring crackled again, and she held up one hand. Amalia fell silent, waiting.

"Nothing about this is going as we were promised," Lady Umber said. "And no, I don't want to hear any more of your excuses. I've sent a group to take possession of the control chamber, so that at least will be under our power."

Jes had used every example of "bad language" she knew on her way into North Waveborn. Now, not one of them felt bad enough for this, not even all of them over and over.

"Amalia, she's sent someone to the control room. As soon as they enter it, it and all these tunnels are going to start to flood."

Expressions of surprise, respect, and then realization chased each other across Amalia's face. "I'll take your pack," she said. She slung it over one shoulder then took Jes's hand. "Let's run."

When she hadn't been walking for hours and hours, Jes could manage a short run without difficulty. Games of tag. One flight of stairs, up or down. She had never seen any use in running just to get from here to there, and she'd carefully avoided any punishment that involved it.

Now, as the light of Amalia's torch flickered off

the stone walls, only her cousin's hand around hers kept Jes going, on and on. The breath started to come from her lungs in painful gasps. There was a stitch in her side, and her legs felt like they were made of lead.

If I stop, I'll drown. That wasn't as much motivation as she'd hoped. Jes tried again. *If I stop, Amalia won't leave me, and* she'll *drown.* Better, but that was wearing down too. *If I stop, there's no one to protect my people.*

It felt like forever, and then there was a rumble of stone shifting. Amalia's hand tightened around hers, and they kept running as the sound of rushing water echoed in the stone tunnels.

The quiet slap of boots on stone was like her heartbeat. When the sound changed, it felt like her heart did, too—splash, slosh. Splash, slosh. The water was up to their ankles. Up to their calves. They could swim, but that would be too slow. Once the tunnels filled, there wouldn't be any air.

The water was up to Jes's waist, chest deep on Amalia, when they spotted the stairs. Amalia continued to drag her forward, even though she was almost underwater herself, and then Amalia was above her, pulling her up, one step at a time, and Jes thought they might make it. A wave of water came thundering down the tunnel, filling it, covering her, and her eyes closed in surprise.

The grip on her hand shifted, became two hands, pulling her through the water, up, up, until her head broke free into air. It was so dark she wasn't certain she had opened her eyes at first, but Amalia was still pulling her up the stairs as the water tried to sweep her away. Her feet settled on the steps, and she was climbing again.

"You—you saved my life," Jes coughed.

"Well, that's what friends are for." Amalia released her hands and patted her on one arm. "Hopefully we can open the trapdoor in the dark."

They walked beside each other, feeling the walls on either side for controls or openings, until Jes clipped her head on the ceiling at the top. The latch was the same as the other two had been, and they eased it up together, climbing out to stand dripping on the stones.

It was dark, but there was enough light to see the figure in front of them, weapon held out to threaten. "Halt, in the name of the king!"

"Chris," Amalia sighed. "It's us."

There was the sound of a gaslight hissing on, and then Jes could see that Amalia was right. Chris sheathed his sword with a sheepish shrug.

"Hey, you were breaking into my castle before dawn. It's my job to keep an eye on things while Mom and Dad are gone."

Jes collapsed on the stone floor in a wet heap. "Of course they are. Did you get sent a regent, too?"

Chris scowled. "Yeah, this grumpy woman called Lady Indigo. I really don't like her."

"Does she have black hair and creepy pale skin and a really sharp nose and chin?" Jes asked.

"And a voice like nails on a chalkboard?" Amalia

added.

"Oh, you've met her!" Chris nodded. "Can't stand her."

Jes shook her head. "I don't buy identical triplets. Something weird is going on. Oh, and whoever they are, they're planning on taking over the islands."

Jes felt her eyes closing while Amalia filled Chris in and then argued with him about the best way of dispatching their foes. After a bit, Amalia shook her awake. "Chris is going to hide us in his top bunk and get us dry clothes. We need to sleep before we try anything else."

How can you hide someone in a top bunk? Jes kept the question to herself, too focused on putting one foot in front of the other. When Chris had snuck them up to his room, the question was answered. The room was a good fifteen feet high, and his bed doubled as a play pirate ship. The top bunk was reached by ladder and was ten feet above the floor, with solid sides to keep someone from falling out ... or anyone below from seeing in.

"Here, towels, night shirts, and just leave your dirty clothes with mine to get washed."

"Won't anyone ask how you got two extra outfits

soaked and dirty over night?" Jes asked.

Chris shrugged. "Not really. That happens at least once a week."

Jes felt like her muscles were turning into jelly. After Chris left to let them change, Amalia stood behind her on the ladder and helped her climb. She was pretty sure she was asleep before she hit the mattress.

Chris brought a picnic basket up into the Crow's Nest—his name for his top bunk—around noon. Jes moaned and covered her head with the nearest pillow until the scents of the food got through to her. "Do you have cinnamon rolls?"

"Cinnamon rolls, meat pies, roasted chicken, some vegetables nobody will eat, cheese, and apples." Chris sounded like someone who had slept a lot longer than either of them had. Jes decided to dive for the basket rather than hit him.

"We can't use the tunnels to get to West Waveborn, and Queen Melia is the last person we have to turn to," Amalia said, grabbing an apple.

Chris frowned. "But there were nine heroes at the beginning. Who were the other two?"

Jes and Amalia turned to look at him. "Nine heroes?" Jes asked.

"That's what the song said. The night before last, Mom was complaining about everything that the song got wrong. It claimed that she and Queen Melia were sorceresses, and Dad was a wizard, and lots of other stupid stuff." Chris shrugged. "The musician that sang it hadn't written it, and I don't know who did write it. But it said nine heroes, and I only know about our parents and Queen Melia. Donal's father wasn't one of them; he and Queen Melia were only married for a couple of months before he decided he wanted to be an explorer more than a prince consort."

"Didn't you ask her or your dad who the other two were?" Amalia demanded.

Chris shrugged again. "I was going to, but then there were these other things like explosives and battles to ask about, and then yesterday morning they left."

Jes brushed her hair back from her face, then stopped. "My earring!"

Chris looked at her like she was crazy, and Amalia explained.

"It was from Queen Melia, and it let Jes listen in to the other one back where the conspirators were."

Chris frowned. "Even if Queen Melia is gone, like our parents, I bet Donal has some way to get in touch with her. We just need to get to him. There's the land bridge, but there's a border crossing partway across."

"How many guards?" Amalia asked, fingering the hilt of her sword.

"Usually two. Mom and Dad would be really mad if we hurt them, though."

Jes imagined her two friends fighting fully grown, armed, trained guards. *What would I be doing? Throwing rocks?* She rubbed her forehead.

"We could take a rowboat, but that's really slow, and somebody would probably see us. Maybe we could stow away on a smuggler's ship."

"Do you really think your parents would allow smugglers to land here?" Amalia argued.

Jes frowned harder, trying to follow some stray thought. Smugglers ...

"Amalia, remember the stories about our great grandfather, Giuseppe?"

Amalia nodded. "A few of them."

Jes turned to Chris. "When he was young, there was a disagreement between his city and the neighboring one, and there were custom stops between them that charged just crazy amounts. Grandfather decided to become a smuggler. Every week he'd go to one custom house with a string of donkeys loaded down with rags and straw. The custom officer would go through everything looking for something of value, but he never found anything, and Grandfather would go home later another way."

"So, what was he smuggling?" Chris asked.

Amalia chuckled. "Donkeys." She turned back to Jes. "You want us to smuggle donkeys?"

Jes shook her head. "I want us to smuggle ourselves."

They didn't even have to wash up for the role, just put on dry clothing and pack laundry bags full of rags. Amalia had kept their packs from completely soaking, so they had the clothing, and Jes's emergency food was still in fair shape.

Amalia argued a little about leaving behind the caltrops and the flask of oil.

"They'll make the customs people nervous," Jes

pointed out. "Besides, I bet Donal has lots of cool gadgets, and I'm sure he'll share."

"I can see the oil," Amalia argued, "but my mini caltrops just look like a game of jacks. If Chris has a rubber ball to put in with them, no one will think twice."

Chris, it turned out, had dozens of rubber balls of different sizes and colors. They were so busy bouncing for a minute that they almost missed the knock on the door.

"Up!" Chris stage whispered and walked slowly and loudly to the door as Jes and Amalia climbed back into the top bunk. Jes peered around a toy cannon and through a porthole in time to see him reach the door and open it.

"Your Highness," a familiar voice said. Jes felt Amalia stiffen beside her. The woman—Lady Indigo—looked just like the other two, and she was frowning down her nose at Chris.

"Yes?" Chris asked.

Lady Indigo bowed. "I just wanted to make sure that you would be present for dinner tonight."

Chris tilted his head. "I never miss meals. Unless I've already eaten them, but usually I'm hungry enough to eat again."

Lady Indigo gave a tiny shrug. "I'll see you tonight, then." She stepped back out and closed the door. There was a tiny clicking noise.

"That's weird," Chris muttered. He shrugged and looked up at them. "So, are we ready to go?"

Amalia stuffed a small red ball into her bag of caltrops. "Mostly. But I think you want to try that door again. I think we've been locked in."

The door was locked. Amalia tried to pick it,
but a bar had been set across the door. They were
well and truly stuck.

They went to the window and looked down.
It was fifty feet down to solid footing, and even
that was a rocky bluff overlooking the sea. Jes felt
queasy and moved back, sitting down on the edge
of Chris's bed.

"There's a window just below, only about eight
feet down," Amalia announced cheerfully. "If it's
unlocked, we can go in that way and escape from
there."

"How are we going to get down?" Chris asked.
"We could take the ladder from the bed, but there

isn't any way to attach it."

"Sheets and pillow cases," Amalia announced. "We tie each set of sheets together long-ways—top sheet to bottom sheet—and then we cross the two sets across each other and tie with the pillow cases to make steps. We just attach the whole thing to the bottom of the bed—easy!"

Jes swallowed. She forced herself to walk over to the window, looked down, and scurried away again. "Amalia ... I can't. I'm sorry."

Amalia looked worried for a moment, then smiled. "That's okay. We won't be able to bring our packs and swords down that way, so Chris and I will go down, break in, and come back up to let you out and get our stuff. You can double check the packing while we're gone."

Chris opened his mouth, and Amalia elbowed him in the ribs. Hard.

"Uh, right. Just as easy to have you wait here," he managed.

Jes felt tears prick her eyes, but she only nodded. *I hate being the weakest one. Slowest runner and the only one afraid of heights. Why would they even want to be friends with me?*

She stayed away from the window as she helped tie off the sheets and double check the connections. In a few minutes, they were ready, and she forced herself back to the window to watch them go.

Watching Amalia take that first step into open air made Jes want to throw up. There were long seconds until her foot found the first cross-tie, and then Amalia grinned and scampered down like a monkey. Chris only waited for her to swing open the lower window and scramble inside before he started down after her. Jes watched as he climbed into the lower room as well. She knelt in front of the window, still looking down, in case they had to come back this way. *And then what will we do?*

A minute passed, and then Chris appeared briefly in the window to give her a thumbs-up. She waved back and then went to the packs, double checking straps and contents. She put on her own to avoid delays and then counted to herself.

Sometime after seven hundred, Jes heard a noise outside the door. She froze, trying to decide if it was worth it to pick up a sword she didn't know how to use. The door slid open, and Amalia peered inside. "Got it! Ready to go?"

The climb had added some extra grime to their hands and faces. Amalia and Chris put on their packs and slid their swords back into the scabbards. With their loads, only someone who knew them would realize they were royalty.

Chris knew the servants' stairs as well as Amalia did in her own home, and they only had to pause twice on their descent to the kitchen level. From there, they took a worn door to the kitchen garden and then out to a dirt trail that led from that servants' entrance into the seaport.

South Waveborn had more trees than Jes was used to, mostly bending trunks with large, broad leaves springing from the tops. Although she knew none of the trees could be much older than she was, they towered above her. *You'd never know that this island was underwater for centuries.*

The harbor was small and sheltered, but they bypassed it altogether, so they only saw the tops of the taller ships. An orange tree, complete with ripe fruit, marked the path to the land bridge.

The land bridge between South Waveborn and West Waveborn was dotted with board and rope bridges over open stretches of water. The bridges swung as the three crossed over, and Jes gripped the sides tightly every time. It wasn't a long way to fall, and she could swim, but the shifting surface was unpleasant. Chris and Amalia appeared to disagree, as they raced each other over every bridge they came to. Jes couldn't bring herself to complain after she'd refused the sheet ladder, so she clung on grimly and kept going.

The actual land parts were boring, barren rocks with some sparse salt grasses and sea birds' nests. The central spire island was like this, just a place for pirates to land. These areas were too small even for that.

"I bet they know we're gone now," Jes said to Amalia. "You and I, that is, since Lady Indigo just saw Chris, but I bet someone realized that at least one of us was long gone. Otherwise, why would they have locked Chris in?"

Amalia frowned. "Maybe. I do take off a lot, but I'm usually there for meals, and this is two I've missed now."

"No one will be looking for the three of us together," Chris said, walking backwards to face them. "The louder we are, the less likely they'll think we have anything to hide."

"Tree, Chris," Jes pointed out. He kept walking backwards, gesturing now with one hand.

"If you want to hide, be conspicuous! That's what Dad says."

"Tree!" Amalia yelled.

"Yeah, like that!" Chris took another step back, slamming into the tree trunk. "Okay, maybe not quite like that."

Jes tried not to laugh, but Amalia and Chris laughed until she had to join in.

"Is that the border stop?" she asked, pointing, when she could talk again.

"Yeah, you can't really call it a house, can you?" There was a single gate across a narrow bit of land, and two bored guards standing on either side of it. The woman who was nearer to them wore a blue uniform, while the man on the other side wore red. They were chatting with each other but stopped as the three of them approached.

"Aren't you supposed to be in school?" the woman asked.

"School break," Jes said brightly. "Mom wanted us out of the house for a bit and sent us to visit Grandma."

"And we didn't do anything!" Amalia chimed in.

"Much," Chris muttered.

The woman quirked a small smile. "Don't leave it too late if you're coming home tonight. No passing after dark."

She stood back, and they walked up to the gate, where the guard in red seemed less happy to see them.

"Anything to declare?" he asked.

They looked at each other and shrugged. "Is it nouns that are declarative or verbs?" Amalia asked. "I get that mixed up."

The man sighed. "Are you bringing anything valuable with you?"

They obediently took off their bags. "This piece of purple might make a doll's dress," Jes pointed out. "It's kind of small, but it's pretty."

"This green is nicer, but I'm too old for dolls," Amalia informed him.

"I never liked dolls much, but I bet you could make a cool flag out of all the pieces," Chris offered.

The man sighed, the woman hid a smile, and the three of them held out their bags expectantly. The man peered and shuffled through each one as though afraid to hurt their feelings by not searching them, then let them on through.

"Go straight to your grandmother's!" he advised.

"We will," Jes lied.

"Ee-yaw," brayed Chris, and Amalia hit him as they walked on, leaving the checkpoint behind.

"Why did you do that?" she hissed.

"Because we're donkeys, and it worked," Chris said, still smiling. "A doll's dress. Really?"

"It would make a very nice doll's dress," Jes said, glowering. "But yes, that worked. Now we only need to make it the rest of the way across without being seen, sneak into the castle, find Donal, and get him to contact his mother."

"And figure out who's trying to steal our islands, and why those three women all look the same, and who they work for, and whether King Gregor actually sent them, and then rescue our parents." Amalia seemed undaunted by the list. "Oh, and find out who the two missing heroes are so they can help us."

"Unless one of them is the villain!" Chris was still bouncy with their success, or the sunlight, or maybe just because he was Chris and he was always like this. Jes sighed as he dashed ahead across the next bridge and Amalia darted after him. Jes followed more slowly, pretending the swaying steps didn't scare her.

They joined a game of dance rope as they crossed the bridge, setting down their laundry bags and going on again without them. Jes spared a thought for the purple fabric that really *would* have been a lovely ball gown for her favorite doll, but there were more important things right now.

The castle on West Waveborn was built onto a cliff top, with buildings following it up the slope as though clinging to its sides. The stone was strange and white, not like the gray of the other three, and it had six spires that rose from towers no wider than a single small room. Jes bit her lip, wondering where to even start looking for Donal.

There was a small explosion from the tower furthest from them, a flash of light followed by smoke. Jes grabbed Amalia's arm and pointed. "He's in there."

Chris raised an eyebrow. "Are you sure?"

Amalia shook her head. "Have you *met* Donal? We're sure."

Donal was small and blond and moved like a ferret who'd been given too much caffeine. He was still smudged with soot when they made it up into his tower, and he barely looked up from his latest experiment.

"Were you expected today? I didn't remember."

Jes took a breath. "No, Donal, we're escaping from evil identical regents who've tricked our parents into leaving."

"That's too bad. Could you hand me that silver wire? No, the other one."

Chris looked ready to explode, but Amalia kicked him and motioned for him to wait. Jes handed over the silver wire.

"Are the regents all pale women with dark hair and sharp features?" Donal asked as he fastened the wire between two parts.

"Yes, that's them."

"Hmm. I did wonder if perhaps Lady Violet wasn't human." Donal tightened a tiny dial. "She's left me alone, so I didn't investigate."

"Has your mother been called away like our parents?" Jes asked, while Amalia clamped a hand over Chris's mouth. Another explosion seemed imminent.

"Yes, yesterday morning. Here, could you give me the notched copper disc from that table?"

Jes handed it over and counted to a hundred. Before she'd quite finished, Donal turned a hidden switch, and the little machine came to life.

"There, that's done. So, do you think Mom is in any danger? Oh, hello, Chris. I didn't see you there."

There were many crucial questions Jes wanted to ask, but Chris blurted out first, "What does that do?"

"It's a voice-activated smoke machine. It should fill a ballroom with thick smoke in under a minute."

Why anyone would want such a thing was a question that could wait. "Yes, your mom could be in danger. We thought, since you two made the earrings for Alex, that you might be able to contact your mom"

Donal frowned. "Unfortunately, we based those on the structures running through the islands. Anywhere on the islands or in the tunnels, they should work fine, but I doubt they'd have more than a few hundred yards of range away from here."

"So, you don't have any way to reach your mother?" Amalia asked.

"I didn't say that. I can track her, which is one option. Taking apart Lady Violet to see what she's up to is another."

Chris and Amalia gripped their swords with matching smiles, and Jes shuddered. "Isn't torture a little … extreme?"

Donal blinked at her. "I wasn't going to torture her. I was going to find her off switch and analyze her programming. It's obvious that she's an android."

"Who can make an android that can pass as a human?" Amalia objected.

"Well, my Uncle Kegan could. At least, he was nearly there the last time I saw him. Some of his machines helped in the fight to raise the islands."

"Eight!" crowed Chris.

"So why isn't he royalty, then?" Jes asked.

"He didn't want it. He told Gregor he'd rather have a good workshop then a kingdom any day." Donal paused as though considering. "I think he was right."

Amalia and Jes shared a look. Gregor had given Kegan a workshop. Kegan knew how to create androids. Gregor had sent four androids to be their regents. It was what Jes's father would call circumstantial evidence, but it didn't look good.

Chris turned at a sound and glanced out the tower window. "Um, Donal? There are six people with weapons headed this way. Is there another way out of here?"

Donal looked up and grimaced. "Oh, I expect Lady Violet went into my study."

Amalia perked up. "Booby traps?"

Donal smiled back. "Several."

Jes held up one hand. "You can talk shop later. Is there a way to avoid bloodshed and dungeons?"

Donal stood up, slipped his latest device into his pocket, and walked across the room. "You're not afraid of heights, are you?"

Terrified. "We'll be fine. Lead the way."

Jes imagined clinging to the sheer wall outside, taking a zip line between towers, or jumping to almost certain death. After refusing the last tower climb, she just hoped that she could jump quickly without having to think about it. In comparison to these thoughts, the spiral slide Donal told them about wasn't nearly as bad.

"It's in the space under the staircases," Donal explained. "More fun, much faster, and an extra way out for emergencies."

Jes could not imagine finding it fun, but she hadn't faced near drowning and Amalia's dozens of traps to back down now. "Lead the way," she repeated and forced herself to sit down on the slide before she could change her mind.

There were muffled sounds above her as Amalia and Chris tried to contain their own glee, but Jes held her breath, counted, and focused on not throwing up. The slide ended at last in a pile of pillows, and she scrambled out of the way before the other two could careen into her.

"So now we can go down into the tunnels, or …" Donal paused at Jes's head shake.

"We had to flood them to prevent the bad guys from sinking the islands."

Donal shrugged. "Well, I had wanted to do some more testing, but I'm sure it's ready."

It was beautiful. Jes stared at the glass and bronze bubble. "It's a miniature airship?"

"Different design, and much smaller. I call it a skiff. Much more versatile, too."

Alex would be so jeal—Jes stopped mid-thought and bit her lip. Was Alex still alive? Were any of their parents?

This workroom—just how many did Donal have?—was underground and opened out mid-cliff.

"You built this?" Amalia asked.

"Oh, Mom helped with this one. I just added some new features."

No wonder people think Queen Melia is a sorceress. I would, too, if I didn't know better.

Chris ticked off his fingers one by one. "We found you, we learned why the regents look the same, we may know who made them, and you can hopefully lead us to your mother and our parents. So, do you know who the ninth hero was?"

Donal shook his head. "Mom doesn't like being called a hero, and neither does my uncle. Was Gregor there? Maybe it was him."

Chris shook his head. "Gregor couldn't investigate. It was a political thing. So, he sent his college friends, and I guess your mother brought along her brother, so that's eight. I just think the ninth might be important."

"I wonder if he or she died, or disappeared like Dark Mathis," Jes offered.

Amalia frowned. "Who was Dark Mathis?"

"The pirate leader? Didn't you hear about him growing up?"

The others shook their heads. "Not by name."

They probably don't have former pirates for their housekeepers. Jes shrugged. "Anyway, are we waiting for dark?"

Donal smiled. "If we did that, they wouldn't have a chance to shoot us down."

"But …" The others were climbing aboard, and Jes followed. From inside, the skiff looked less like a child's toy and more like a fairy-tale carriage. It also looked about as sturdy as a soap bubble.

I don't think it's heights I'm afraid of, just falling, Jes reassured herself. She followed Donal's example and strapped herself in, then took a deep breath.

The skiff was nearly soundless, so quiet that for a moment she could make out each of their breathing. Then it slipped out the hidden tunnel in the cliff and into open air.

Even though it looked like she was sitting mid-air, Jes found that the height didn't bother her at all. The ships below in the sea looked like toys, and the ocean was made of a dozen shades of blue and gray.

"Airship on your six," Chris warned.

"Another approaching on your nine," Amalia added.

Jes looked around, trying to figure out what they meant. *Who gives directions by pretending that they're sitting in the middle of a giant clock? My friends, that's who.*

"Does this thing have weapons?" Amalia asked, a hopeful lilt to her voice.

"No. Mom is super stingy with weapons. But we won't need any."

"But you said they'd shoot us out of the sky," Jes protested.

"Well, I'm sure they'll *try*." Donal sounded far too cheerful as he operated the controls, and Jes thought it likely that her peaceful ride was about to be ruined.

The sun was setting behind the castle so that as they moved, they went from bands of bright light to bands of shadow.

"Incoming!" Chris yelled, and Jes jumped, despite the harness. Donal adjusted the controls, and they jerked to one side. It felt to Jes like her stomach had been left behind. The air where they had been the moment before erupted in flame and shrapnel.

"Close enough," Donal said cheerfully and pushed the controls all the way forward. They slanted toward the blue gray waves, faster and faster, and Jes smothered a whimper, closing her eyes just before they hit.

There was a slight impact, and then Jes opened her eyes again to confirm that they were still alive. "Wait, this thing goes underwater?" A spotlight lit up their path. The harbor was deeper than she'd expected, although a shipwreck was impaled upon a rocky spire to one side. A school of blue and yellow fish darted out of their way.

"This is the coolest thing ever!" Amalia crowed.

"I want one," Chris nodded. "But it needs weapons."

Donal grinned. "It has other things, though." He hit a button, and pieces of twisted metal rose up beside them, headed for the surface. "Now they'll be sure they got us."

"Where to now?" Jes asked. She watched the fish go by through the glass. Water was so much calmer than dropping out of the sky.

"Mom is east-northeast, so somewhere on the mainland. Probably near the capitol city, where my uncle lives."

Amalia and Jes exchanged glances again. "Do your mom and your uncle get along well?" Amalia asked.

"Yeah, pretty much," Donal answered, adjusting their course. "We only see him a couple of times a year, but he's pretty cool. He likes to make things like I do."

Since you couldn't even talk to Donal when he

was in the middle of a project, that didn't guarantee that Kegan and Queen Melia were close. On the other hand, Donal was a great friend once you got his attention. Jes shook her head. There were too many questions and not enough answers.

Donal pointed out the weird crystalline vents that powered the islands when they rose and fell. "My uncle has been studying them in between all his other projects. Imagine what we could do with that kind of technology!"

Jes bit her lip. *Lady Umber knew how to raise and lower the islands. Where else could she have learned that?*

An airship would have been faster, but Donal's skiff could beat every surface ship she'd ever seen. The water looked darker and more dangerous after the sun had fully set, and Donal piloted them past shadows just beyond the spotlight's reach that could have been reefs or sea monsters.

She drifted off to sleep, and when she woke, she saw that Amalia and Chris were asleep, too. Donal still piloted the skiff, his eyes intent. Jes unstrapped and made her way forward.

"Can you teach me how to pilot?" she whispered.

Donal grinned. "Sure," he whispered back. "It's pretty easy. Pull back to go up, push forward to go down. This lever on the left to go left, this lever on the right to go right."

He unstrapped and moved over for her to take his place. Jes sat down and grasped the controls gingerly, then a little more firmly as she felt them vibrate. She made tiny changes experimentally, enjoying the sense of control.

"You have to really watch the edges of your light so you're prepared to adjust before you have to." Donal helped her navigate around a reef, then sat back and watched her. A large object in front of them moved out of their way just as Jes was about to go around it. She stared after it for a moment, open mouthed, then looked ahead again.

"What was that?"

Donal shrugged. "Big shark, small whale, baby sea monster. We don't look like food, so nothing is likely to bother us."

Jes shuddered. The water didn't seem quite as soothing, but it was still fun to feel in charge.

"Do you want a nap?" she asked. "I'll wake you if

anything gets interesting."

Donal checked a few instruments, then nodded. "We'll be getting to the mainland just before dawn. I'll set an alarm for a bit out so we can all wake up and get ready."

He went back to her seat and strapped in. In a few minutes, his breathing had slowed to match Amalia and Chris. Jes looked out into the endless dark beyond her spotlight and maneuvered the skiff from side to side.

Reefs rose up from one side or another, and fish big and little darted out of the light as she approached. Once, a mass much larger than the last creature moved directly in front of her, and she moved north as it shifted south. An enormous eye just caught the light as she skimmed on by. *Not a baby this time.* It was both terrifying and oddly peaceful to venture on like this. *If I knew my people were safe, I'd be happy doing this.*

It was a little over twenty-four hours since the controls had flooded. Lady Umber and the others couldn't close the vents until they closed the doors that had flooded the tunnels. They might have ways to go underwater—did androids need to breathe, and did water hurt them?—and she had to assume that they knew how to fix everything she'd done. Draining the water without the vents help would take time, and it would take even more time to build the pressure up in the vents. If they were completely on top of things, they could sink her island in just over another twenty-four hours. Half the time she'd delayed them was already gone.

By the time the alarm woke the others, she'd made some hard decisions.

"Saving our parents has to be our second priority," she said firmly as Donal took the controls back from her. "We have to stop the androids from sinking our islands."

Chris opened his mouth to argue, then shut it. Amalia scowled, but nodded. Donal frowned.

"I'd say that Mom was the best person to stop them, but it's true that Uncle Kegan would be just as useful."

Jes took a deep breath. "Donal, what if your uncle was the one who built the androids?"

Donal tilted his head as though thinking. "He might have built them. I don't think he would have planned for them to be used this way. But if he did, then he's the most important person to stop. Either way, I think we should go to him first."

Amalia nodded, one hand on the hilt of her sword. "So, can you get us there without being seen?"

Donal nodded. "Uncle Kegan's workshop is right off the Silent River. I can get us right to his back door."

The Silent River split off from the Song River just east of the capital and traveled straight from there to the sea. It was not, Donal informed them, especially quiet, but it lacked all the waterfalls and sharp turns and unexpected shallows of the Song. This made it perfect for an approach by the skiff.

They moored the craft by the river's edge, just as the sky was turning red. After they had all clambered ashore, Donal sank the skiff down to the bottom of the river so no early morning craft would run aground on it.

While South Waveborn had seemed strange to Jes because of its trees, and West Waveborn because of its white stone castle, the mainland was just alien.

Dozens of different types of birds flew and called around them, and odd furred mammals scurried by in the underbrush. Plant life was everywhere, and thickets and trees crowded directly up to the water's edge.

Donal led the way through a series of hedges that he explained was a maze. "The key is just one seventh expressed as a decimal," he explained, "starting with right." He sighed at their blank looks. "Point one four two eight and so on. First right, fourth left—easy."

They just followed him, not arguing the point. The maze led them to a back door that was locked.

"I'm sure I have explosives on me," Donal muttered.

Amalia pulled a pin from her hair. "Let's save the explosives for after they know we're here."

I am the most boring person in the whole world, Jes decided. *I don't swordfight, I don't blow things up, and I don't know how to pick locks.* At least the last was something she might be interested in learning.

She was reminded of something she did do well when they got inside and the others' shoes and boots clattered. She put a finger to her lips and crept silently to the first corner. A quick look, and she crept back.

"Okay, I think there are guards."

"People?" Chris whispered back.

"Spiders. Large mechanical spiders."

Donal looked thoughtful, but Amalia and Chris both smiled. Chris pulled his sword free. "Perfect."

I don't even see any rocks to throw. Jes followed reluctantly as Amalia and Chris charged around the corner.

The six spiders were the size of dinner platters. They also shot webs. Amalia and Chris both ducked the streams sent toward them, and their swords struck with a clatter of metal on metal.

"Those webs may be a problem," Donal commented, rummaging through his pockets. "Here, a short-distance flamer."

Jes caught the toss easily and then darted up as a web ensnared Chris's right leg. She flicked the flamer on, burning through the thick strand between his leg and the wall. Chris charged in further, already hitting a second spider.

Donal used a different device to cut the webbings from Amalia's sword arm. The spiders chittered together—*communicating?*—then the remaining three backed up.

"Oh, no you don't," Amalia said, her eyes blazing. She grinned like a maniac as she raced forward, bringing her sword down to cut one in half. The other two webbed both her arms, and her smile turned to a look of intense irritation. "Seriously?"

Chris darted in, stopping the spiders from biting her, while Donal and Jes moved forward to free her arms. Then, Chris took the spider on the left while Amalia took the one on the right, and then there were only mechanical parts left littering the floor.

Jes slipped the flamer into her pocket. "It doesn't look like your uncle wants company," she commented.

Donal nodded. "This isn't really like him. I'm getting a little worried."

Jes snorted. "Androids, airships, and treason … and *now* you're a little worried?"

Donal shrugged. "No sense borrowing trouble."

Amalia and Chris kept their swords out and ready as they went forward. After the fight, sneaking in quietly seemed a lot less likely. The door at the end of the corridor was also locked, and once again, Amalia opened it.

The workroom beyond the door looked like a combination of a toyshop and a murder scene. Android parts, disturbingly lifelike, littered shelves and tables, with gadgets in various states of disrepair in between them. At the far end, a tall, slender man with spiky blond hair and goggles was putting pieces together with total attention.

"Uncle Kegan?" Donal asked. "What are you doing?"

The man didn't look up. "Donal, lad, was I expecting you? Sorry, I have this important project to finish for a friend. You won't mind waiting, will you? It should only be a few more hours."

Judging by the scattered plates of crumbs, the project had already been going on for several days. Jes cleared her throat, but Amalia spoke first.

"Actually, there's a bit of a problem. Aside from your leaving spiders to attack us and sending androids to take over our kingdoms, that is."

"Attack? Take over? That doesn't sound right. I'm sure we can sort it all out as soon as I finish this for my friend Mathis. He needs it today for the party Gregor is throwing. Or maybe Mathis is throwing the party for Gregor. I'm not clear on that part." He still hadn't looked up, and Jes sympathized with Chris, who looked ready to scream.

"Mathis?" Jes asked. "Your friend is Dark Mathis, the pirate?"

Kegan finally looked up. "Oh, no, that was years ago. Nobody is to know that. They'd lock him up or kill him, and we agreed that he'd get another chance instead."

Chris crowed suddenly. "He's the ninth hero!"

Kegan fluttered his hands like they didn't quite belong to him. "Well, really, none of us felt like heroes. But yes, when we decided that he wasn't a bad fellow, that he had treated his crew well and didn't deserve to die—well, the only way out was to pretend he had been one of us."

Kegan picked up a screwdriver and gestured with it. "The attacks were almost entirely on Alsandian ships, and Mathis told us that he'd been paid by a few of the surrounding countries to carry them out. We held him off at the tiny central island until Melia raised the islands, and that broke two of his ships and beached the last. He couldn't get away, and if we brought him back in chains, the whole story would have gotten out. There might have been war. So, it was either kill him right there and then or save him. He came back here with me to learn about steam technology and other fascinating stuff, and he's been a perfect gentleman for the last eighteen years."

Jes sighed. "Did he ask you to make four androids for him? Tall, pale women with black hair and sharp features?"

Kegan nodded, then shook his head. "Five, actually. They're a surprise for Gregor. All of this is a surprise for Gregor, for the party. To make it up to him, Mathis said."

Jes saw when the realization came to each of the others. "Kegan, Mathis is going to assassinate Gregor. And he's going to set himself up as King of the Waveborn Islands."

Kegan opened his mouth as though to argue, then closed it again. "Oh, dear," he said.

"We need to stop it. Where is this happening and when?"

"Across town, at Darrius Hall." He looked over at a clock. "In about an hour."

"They'll never let us in. We look like street urchins with good teeth and swords. We don't have time to both change and get there, even if we had appropriate clothing to change into." Jes rubbed her forehead.

Amalia paced. "Too many guards to fight our way in. Is there any way to sneak in?"

"Sewers?" Chris asked. "Every place has sewers."

Sewers ... water ... Darrius Hall. "Isn't there a huge water garden in Darrius Hall? Alex mentioned that she was looking forward to seeing it."

Kegan nodded. "Enormous indoor waterfall. There's a faint mist inside most of the time."

"The water has to come from somewhere. Is it

near the river?" Jes turned to Donal. "Do you think the skiff would fit?"

"Only one way to find out." Donal frowned intently. "It's worth a try."

"What are you planning?" Kegan asked, perplexed.

"Adventure," Chris assured him. "The very best kind."

Amalia, Chris, and Donal scoured the workshop for useful things while Jes tried to explain the plan to Kegan. Fortunately, impulsiveness ran in the family, because he just nodded and grabbed his coat. Jes threw on a cloak, and then they were ready.

The way out was far less eventful, although Kegan was disturbed at the evidence that Mathis had set the spiders to attack anyone who might disturb—*or warn*—him. "But he's been such a good friend. Always found me parts, never made me leave off inventing to go be social ..."

The skiff distracted him, and he and Donal talked about the craft while they boarded and then took it underwater again. The Hall was upriver, on the opposite side, and within a few minutes, they found a huge underwater vent with an inflow pipe beside it. This, aggravatingly, had a sturdy grate over it, and in the interest of time, they agreed that Donal could use explosives to unmount the grate. The ripples from the explosion rocked them back a bit, but they were able to enter the pipe and follow it upward.

Time was passing, and Jes found herself checking Kegan's watch over and over again. When the pipe divided, they took the larger branch. Soon, the rush of water was such that Donal had to set the engines on reverse to slow them down so he could steer—and, if necessary, stop. The noise outside became louder, the motion more turbulent, and then, for one instant, they were suspended in open air.

They were in an enormous room. Across from them was a balcony with a dozen people on it. Below them, the fifth android pointed a gun at a tall man in a crown. Crowds of people watched in dismay. Jes blinked, and then they were falling, plummeting, landing in a wave of water that sent the crowned man back and knocked the android over.

"Everybody out!" Donal shouted, hitting the lever to open the door. Jes scrambled out of her harness, but Amalia and Chris were already out, swords brandished. She ducked out between Donal and Kegan, splashing through the waist-deep water toward the crowd.

Amalia and Chris had taken up positions in front of the king like bodyguards, and Jes looked around wildly. She knew Dark Mathis had to be here, but what did he look like?

Lady Whatever was staggering to her feet, soaked from the waist down, but her grasp on the gun was steady. "Three for the price of one," she said coolly, pointing.

Kegan ran up and grabbed the android's arm. She lifted the arm and flung him away while transferring the gun to her other hand, her gaze never wavering. Kegan landed against a pillar and groaned.

Jes felt the world narrow. *You will always know one good thing to do.* She felt in her pocket and pulled out the flamer. The android's clothing was soaked, but her hair …

Even wet, her boots were quiet on the stone floor. One step closer, another, a third. She lifted the flamer, pushed it on, and held it to the android's thick braid.

For a moment, nothing happened, and then the flame spread up the black hair like a sunrise lighting a mountain. The android tilted her head slightly, as though aware of a problem she couldn't identify, and then her hand with the gun fell as she began to twitch. Her head was melting, features blurring into each other. In another few seconds, she was on the floor, the flames sizzling as they met the puddles around them.

There was shocked silence for a long moment, and then the sound of clapping. Jes looked up to see a pale man with black hair and a beard on a balcony above them.

"Oh, bravo. Or brava, perhaps, for some of you. Nicely done, but I can't have my grand revenge stolen so easily, even if I can't pin it all on poor Kegan there. Soldiers? Shoot them."

Donal shouted and threw something, not toward Dark Mathis, but toward the king. Smoke spewed out from it instantly. Even as the soldiers on the balcony lifted guns, they vanished from view.

Donal grabbed her arm, handing a wobbly Kegan off to her as he led them to the others and out of the room. There was shouting around them, but she ignored it as Donal took them through a low grate she hadn't noticed. It opened onto a passageway.

There was a staircase down in front of her, unnerving in the dark, but someone was in front of her, and she just counted her steps as she supported Kegan down the stairs. Eighteen, twenty-four, thirty, thirty-six … and she was on a level surface. She moved forward carefully with Kegan until she found a wall to her right to let him lean against.

There was a scraping sound from behind her, and a flickering light appeared in the darkness. Donal, Amalia, Chris, Kegan, and the king stood in a round chamber with high walls, a staircase at one end, and an archway at the other. The archway was set with fancy projecting bricks. It towered over them, maybe fifteen feet high, and the ceiling was even higher than that. Donal's candle didn't reach to the darkness beyond. Jes leaned against the corner, out of the way, and caught her breath.

"Your Majesty?" Donal asked politely. "Do we hide here, or is there a good way out?"

"It opens up ahead. There's a hidden stair to the balcony, but I'd recommend that we let the trained professionals take on the people up there." Gregor sighed. "Thank you, by the way. Once this is settled, I'd love to know why—and how—you came here."

There was a sound from the darkness, then a circle of light, and Dark Mathis appeared around the corner, gun drawn in his right hand, his left holding a torch. "That would be fascinating, but unfortunately, all of our curiosities will have to go unsatisfied. It's time for the final act of my grand revenge."

Amalia and Chris still had their swords out, but he could take them both out before they reached him. *Maybe if we all rushed him, one or two of us would make it.* Jes looked at the arch again. He hadn't seen her. He was standing just below the center of the arch.

"Why revenge?" Amalia asked. "It doesn't seem grand at all. It seems rather petty. Oh, boo-hoo, Gregor's friends stopped me from pirating, gave severance pay to my crew, and failed to imprison or execute me. It's just not fair, my life is over. Seriously, what have you got to even be *annoyed* about?" Amalia put her free hand on her hip and shook her head. "And my parents say *I* can be unreasonable."

It was too high. *I can't. I just can't.* Jes took a silent breath and put one booted foot up on the lowest stone.

Chris was talking, but Jes couldn't stop to look. "She's got a point. I mean, I'd never even *heard* of you, so how important could you be? Especially if nobody even put you in jail?"

For a moment, there was silence. Jes grabbed the blocks above and kept climbing. "How could children like you possibly understand?" Mathis exploded.

Gregor cleared his throat. "I'm afraid I don't understand either," the king apologized. "It all does seem a bit like a temper tantrum."

Jes's eyes threatened to cross when she looked down, but she was above the pirate now. She held on with one hand as she unfastened her cloak with the other. A drop of water fell from it, hitting Mathis in the forehead. He started to look up, and she dropped the cloak onto him.

The torch sizzled as the wet cloak doused it, then Donal blew out his own candle as Amalia and Chris rushed forward. Everything was dark, scrabbling, and swearing from the darkness that might have been Mathis but sounded like Gregor.

Jes held on with both hands to the stones of the archway. There was a squeal that sounded like Chris, the noisy patter of shoes on stone, and then the familiar scrape of flint on steel. A small circle of light showed Donal holding the gun while Chris and Amalia held blades at the ready over the kneeling pirate.

Below her, Mathis was holding a candle, pointing at Gregor as though his free hand still held a weapon. "You—you idealistic idiots! Calm and understanding and always taking the higher ground! You've just never cared enough about something to kill for it!"

A dark object connected with the back of his head with a crack, and the pirate slumped to the floor. Chris dove for the candle as it rolled out of his hand and held it aloft.

"That's where you'd be wrong," a familiar voice said grimly.

"Daddy?"

King Willem took a step further into the room and looked up at Jes. "Hello, Peanut. How did you get up there?"

"You didn't kill him, did you, Willem? There will be so much more paperwork if he's dead." Jes's mother came into view behind him.

"I'll do the paperwork," Alex volunteered. "Or we

could just let Uncle Phineas carry him. It wouldn't be his fault if he dropped him. Down a flight of stairs. Repeatedly."

"Are you all here? Our parents, too?" Amalia asked.

"All of us." Jes's mother smiled. "We'll have stories to share, after everything's settled."

Jes's father never took his eyes from hers. "First, I think, we have to get Jes down. Do you want to climb, honey?"

Jes's father was the tallest person in the room. It was still a long way down to him, but not as far away as the floor. "Catch me?" Jes asked.

Her father opened his arms and smiled. "Always."

After Dark Mathis and his mercenaries from the balcony had been dragged off to jail, they gathered in Gregor's library for a late breakfast. Soldiers had been sent to clear the islands of conspirators, and Jes felt almost like the whole thing had been a dream. Except that she was tired, starving, and badly in need of a bath.

"We would have been in trouble if Willem hadn't insisted on seeing the life jackets before we took off. They'd been moved to someplace you couldn't reach while the airship was in the air, and in retrospect that should have made us all a bit suspicious. But we had them, and even when we were hit, the Captain managed to slow our descent so that we could escape the ship when it landed in the water. The life jackets kept us afloat so that we could cobble a raft from the wreckage. It still took us a long time to get to shore, and then it was to a little island off the mainland. We left the crew and captain there when we took off again to go for help—a few of them had gotten hurt helping us and were in no condition to be moved again. Then we got to the mainland and discovered that there was no word of a conference, but we did hear about some people being kept in a smuggler's den."

"That was us," Aunt Anya confirmed. "All the rest of us, so apparently, we weren't considered dangerous enough to kill. Possibly because Willem was the only one who really argued for executing Mathis, back at the beginning."

"Was I wrong?" Jes's father asked.

Aunt Anya grimaced. "I guess not."

"We had just gotten ourselves free when we

met the three of them coming to rescue us," Queen Melia added. "From there, we were going to warn Gregor that something was terribly wrong and then get back to all of you."

Uncle Darby took a swallow of his drink. "We were about five minutes too late. But fortunately, you were right on time."

Gregor sighed. "I'm in your debt, again. I wish I had thought to invite you all here for a visit." He brightened. "Well, you're here now. Why don't we just start today?"

"Oh, but—" Jes broke off, blushing.

"But," Gregor prompted her gravely.

"I really need to get home to make sure my people are safe. After that, I'd love to come back for a visit."

Gregor looked at her for a long minute. "We'll arrange that." He looked over at her parents. "I'm sorry," he said.

Mom shook her head. "Don't be. Some people are suited to it."

It was a strange conversation, but Jes focused on the part she understood.

"Can I go home soon? Now?"

"Now," Gregor agreed. "You can come back for the visit when you're sure everything is settled."

Mrs. Clemens hugged her so hard that she could barely breathe. "Well done, Princess Jes."

Nickname *and* title. Jes thought she could live with that.

"Was anyone hurt? Are you all safe?"

Mrs. Clemens smiled. "It only took us a day to figure out who the people reporting to that creature were. Then we locked them up, and her little worm of a secretary, and her. The soldiers who came switched her off and took her apart, and took the others off to jail. It wasn't a pretty thing to see, even though we already knew that she couldn't be human from the way she kept trying to beat down the door hour after hour. If we hadn't tricked her inside, I don't think we'd have been able to contain her."

Jes smiled. "Mrs. Clemens, I think you have to be the one in charge whenever the family can't be here. No one else is as amazing as you are."

The housekeeper turned pink, but Mom and Dad nodded their agreement.

They stayed long enough to tell her the whole

story, and for baths, and for Alex to pack replacement dresses for all those lost at sea. Jes let her mother pack for her, just insisting that a clean pair of boots be included.

She settled back on her sister's bed, watching Alex pack once again. "I'm sorry about your earring."

Alex hugged her. "Silly. As though an earring mattered more than you do."

"Do you still think you want to stop being a princess, after all of this?"

Alex laughed. "Now more than ever. But I've always known."

Jes frowned. "How can you? I don't have any idea."

"Jes, you've always known, too. What was the first thing you did when you found out that those people were going to use you as a puppet and possibly hurt the people who live here?"

Jes paused. "I made sure they couldn't."

Alex nodded. "And the first thing you thought of when the crisis was over? Checking to make sure your people were safe. It's not something I want, Jes, but it almost doesn't matter if you want it or not. It's something you are."

Responsibility. And fighting her own battles, which might involve numbers or conversations instead of swords but would still be important. Jes imagined the wandering under the water, and the same thought came to her. *I could be happy, if I knew my people were safe.*

She hugged Alex. "Thank you."

Alex laughed. "Hey, this time you'll be coming with me."

Jes nodded. It would be fun, going back to the mainland without androids and pirates to fight. The best part, though, would be coming home again afterwards.

About the Author

Hope Erica Schultz writes science fiction and fantasy stories and novels for kids, teens, and adults. Her first novel, the YA post-apocalyptic *Last Road Home*, came out in 2015, and she was co-editor of the YA anthology *One Thousand Words for War*, in 2016. Her stories have appeared in multiple anthologies and magazines.